Out There?

MYSTERIOUS ENCOUNTERS

John Townsend

Raintree

Chicago, Illinois

For information, address the publisher:
Raintree, 100 N. LaSalle, Suite 1200, Chicago, IL 60602

Printed and bound in China
08
10 9 8 7 6 5 4 3 2

Library of Congress Cataloging-in-Publication Data
Townsend, John.
  Mysterious encounters / John Townsend.
    p. cm. -- (Out there)
Summary: Explores reports of mysterious objects that have landed on earth, from "frozen water meteorites" to live pink frogs to UFOs, as well as what may still be heading this way.
Includes bibliographical references and index.
  ISBN 1-4109-0563 2 (lib. binding), 1-4109-0964-6 (Pbk.)
  ISBN 978-1-4109-0563-5 (lib. binding), 978-1-4109-0964-0 (Pbk.)
  1. Human-alien encounters--Juvenile literature. 2. Unidentified flying objects--Juvenile literature. 3. Curiosities and wonders--Juvenile literature. [1. Human-alien encounters. 2. Unidentified flying objects. 3. Science--Miscellanea. 4. Curiosities and wonders.] I. Title. II. Series.
  BF2050.T69 2004
  001.94--dc21
                        2003010731

Acknowledgments
The publisher would like to thank the following for permission to reproduce photographs: Pp. 4–5 Frank Zullo/Science Photo Library; pp.6, 46 (bottom) Science Photo Library; pp. 7 (left), 13, 14 (top), 19, 20 (bottom), 25, 26, 34, 36, 43 (top), 44 (left), 45 Fortean Picture Library; 7 (right) Tom Bean/Corbis; pp. 8, 18 (left), 22 (right), 46 (top), 51 Photodisc; pp. 8–9 Chris Madeley/Science Photo Library; p. 9 Michael Dunning/Science Photo Library; p. 10 (top), 10 (3rd from top) Steve Benbow; pp. 11 (left), 15, 20 (top), 32 (right), 35, 38 (right) Mary Evans Picture Library; p. 11 (right) Gregory Scott/Science Photo Library; p. 12 Owen Franken/Corbis; p. 14 (bottom), 41 Ronald Grant Archive; pp. 16, 17 Rex Features; pp. 16–17 Peter Finger/Corbis; pp. 18 (right), 26–27, 40 (left), 47 Alamy Images; p. 21 First Light/Corbis; 22 (left) USAF; p. 23 Bettman/Corbis; pp. 10 (2nd from top), 10 (4th from top) 24, 39, 44 (right) Corbis; p. 27 Randy Wells/Corbis; p. 28 (right) George Hall/Corbis; p. 28 (left) Matthew Mcvay/Corbis; p. 29 Howard Davies/Corbis; pp. 30, 30–31, 31, 36–37 40 (right), 42, 48 (left), 49 Kobal Collection; p. 33 Gettty Images Taxi; p. 38 (left) Getty Images Imagebank; p. 43 (bottom) NASA; p. 48 (right) Roger Ressmeyer/Corbis; p. 50 European Space Agency.
Cover photograph used with permission of Topham Picturepoint.

CONTENTS

Some words are shown in bold, **like this.** You can find out what they mean by looking in the glossary. You can also look out for them in the "Weird Words" box at the bottom of each page.

ARE WE ALONE?

UFOS

A UFO is simply an **unidentified** flying object. That just means something in the sky that cannot be explained. The term *UFO* was first used in the middle of the last century, but strange things in the sky go back to the beginning of recorded history. Sometimes there is a simple solution and sometimes there is not.

The sky has always amazed us. It is not just its changing moods, strange colors, and mysterious clouds. We are also puzzled by what falls from the sky. Sometimes strange things can drop to Earth.

Many people dream of other worlds above the clouds. But it is the sky at night that holds real magic. We look up at the stars and wonder about the many things that we cannot explain. We have asked the same questions for centuries: What is out there in the universe? Are we alone? Some people claim to know the answers. They say they have met other **beings** from beyond the sky. Have these **encounters** really happened?

Many people claim they have had a close encounter of some kind. Is this just nonsense? Read on and find out. >>

WEIRD WORDS

alien creature from a far-away place or another planet
being living creature

DIFFERENT ENCOUNTERS

Mysterious encounters come in four types. They can involve seeing UFOs, **aliens,** or mysterious markings.

- **Close Encounters of the first kind.**
  This is a sighting of a strange object.

- **Close Encounters of the second kind.**
  This is when a UFO leaves marks or has some effect that can be measured.

- **Close Encounters of the third kind.**
  This is when an alien makes some sort of contact with humans.

- **Close Encounters of the fourth kind.**
  This is when an alien kidnaps a human.

FIND OUT LATER...

Is this mysterious object real or fake?

Were these marks made by UFOs?

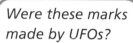

Has anyone really been kidnapped by aliens?

encounter meeting, especially an unexpected one
unidentified something that cannot be named or explained

FALLING FROM THE SKY

ICE BOMBS

When lumps of ice fall from the sky, people often blame aircraft restrooms— even though aircraft restrooms are never emptied in the sky. But reports of falling ice go back hundreds of years. Some scientists think that thousands of ice lumps from space hit Earth each year.

All through history people have reported strange things falling to Earth. Why does it sometimes rain frogs or crabs? A shower of sardines has even been known to fall into the street.

- In 1974 cans and bottles fell onto houses for four hours in New Zealand.
- In 1979 a gooey blob fell into a garden in Canada. It was hot and smoking.
- In 1980 three umbrellas fell from a clear blue sky in South Africa.

Perhaps the wind scoops these things up into the sky. **Waterspouts** may suck creatures up into the clouds and drop them inland.

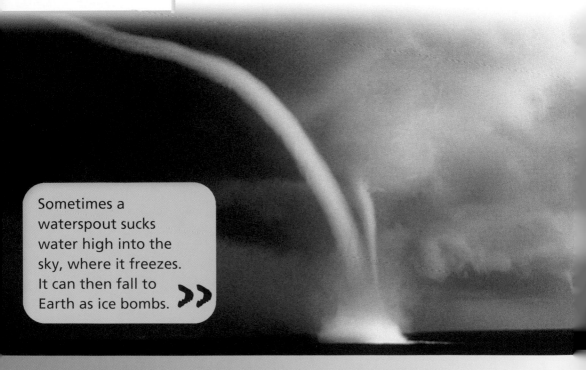

Sometimes a waterspout sucks water high into the sky, where it freezes. It can then fall to Earth as ice bombs. ❯❯

WEIRD WORDS meteorite lump of rock, metal, or matter from outer space
space junk pieces of old satellites and spacecraft

CLOSE SHAVES

Objects fall from the sky all the time. Some can be explained, but many cannot. With all the aircraft and **space junk** up above, it is not surprising that pieces fall to Earth. Plastic may melt as it falls and then hit the ground in weird shapes. Some green blobs have appeared in people's gardens as **unidentified** falling objects.

Many stories tell of blocks ice falling from the sky. A man in Russia had a close call in the 1990s when a big lump of ice fell at his feet. He took it home to keep in his freezer. Scientists said it was a frozen water **meteorite.**

MORE ICE FALLS

- In 1984 a 5-foot- (1.5-meter-)wide ice bomb fell on a house in Great Britain. It smashed through the roof.
- In 1985 an ice block the size of a grand piano crushed a fence in Connecticut.

Hail stones can be enormous—and dangerous!

In 1987 it rained tiny pink frogs in England. They had come from Africa.

STRANGE LIGHTS

People have always looked up at mysterious lights in the sky and wondered what it all means. We now know more about shooting stars and **comets** moving through the night sky. Just imagine what people thought about them hundreds of years ago. Strange lights in the sky still puzzle and often scare people.

Colored moving lights at the North and South Poles have always been mysterious. People used to think they were signs from the gods. Now we know about magnetic dust from the Sun that glows with gases high in the earth's **atmosphere.** It is called the northern lights, or aurora borealis. The southern lights are the aurora australis.

Is this ball lightning? Or something more mysterious?

AURORA

An aurora is a fantastic light show in the sky. It beats any laser display! Auroras can last for hours during the night. They light up the sky with amazing, swirling colors. Before people understood what they were, they were often terrified.

comet moving body in space with a bright head and a long tail

BALL LIGHTNING

Floating balls of light that fall from the sky and chase people may seem to come from **science fiction**. But such things really have been seen and filmed. They are called **ball lightning** because they can arrive with storms. Some have shot into people's houses in a shower of sparks.

Ball lightning is like a soccer ball of bright light and energy that floats and fizzes just above the ground. It is very rare, and scientists have been unable to study exactly what it is. It has even been blamed for setting people on fire and has been described as a mysterious power from space.

METEORS

Meteors are rocks, or "space dust," that burn up as they fall through Earth's atmosphere. Meteors flare across the sky at night and are also called shooting stars. Meteor showers happen at certain times of the year. These showers can create more than 70 shooting stars every hour.

Meteors have often been mistaken for spaceships. ❱❱

ENCOUNTERS OF THE FIRST KIND

COMMON VIEWS ON UFOS

Falling objects and lights cannot always be explained. When there is no explanation, they are called UFOs. Less than 60 years ago, the U.S. Air Force first used the term *UFO* for anything seen in the sky that could not be recognized. Since then, most people tend to think of a UFO as a spaceship from another world.

In fact, over 200 different objects have been mistaken for **alien craft.** Everything from weather balloons to aircraft lights to meteors to owls glowing in the dark have been reported to the police. Yet there are cases on record where no good reason was ever found for mysterious objects in the sky.

UFOs are real. I believe aliens come down to visit us.

There is life out there, but it is too far away to worry about.

There are no such things as aliens.

You can't be sure. Maybe. Maybe not.

What do *you* think?

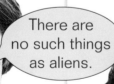

DOES IT MATTER? WHO CARES?!

WEIRD WORDS **alien craft** spaceship flown by creatures from another planet
invade to enter somewhere and take over

SAUCERS

Mysteries in the sky go back thousands of years. **Prehistoric** cave carvings in Hunan, China, show pictures of objects that look like spacecraft. People in Japan have reported glowing shapes in the sky for 800 years. Five hundred years ago, a sailor on board Columbus's ship, the *Santa Maria,* recorded a shining shape in the sky.

It was not until 1947 that such shapes were called "flying saucers." Kenneth Arnold, a pilot from Idaho, saw nine silver disks over Mount Rainier in Washington State. He judged their speed to be 1,200 miles (1,930 kilometers) per hour. He said they looked like "pie plates skipping over the water." The name stuck. Since then, the media has used the label "flying saucer."

SMALLEST UFO

Did you know that insects have often been mistaken for UFOs? Fireflies attract each other with a flashing light under their bodies. People seeing these flashing lights floating over the ground in the distance have thought they were alien **invaders.**

This UFO was photographed near an airbase in New Mexico.

THE MYSTERY AIRSHIP

In 1896 a bright light appeared in dark clouds over California and moved slowly west over the rooftops. Hundreds of people saw it. In the next day's newspaper, the headline read: "Hundreds claim they saw flying airship." It was the first time the word *airship* had been used. It would be another seven years before the first airplane flight.

Over the next weeks, thousands of people saw the "airship," from San Francisco to Chicago.

So what was it? Had someone made a secret aircraft? Or was it the planet Venus, which was shining brightly over the United States at that time? Many **astronomers** think it was an **encounter** of the Venus kind!

April 23, 2000
Nevada

A passenger in a plane flying from Denver, Colorado, to San José, California, reported a round, silver object with a domed top speeding below the aircraft. He said the UFO was about 50 ft (16 m) across and moving at 3,000 mi (4,800 km) per hour.

Modern airships, or **blimps,** are seen floating above cities to advertise events or products. But they travel very slowly. »

astronomer someone who studies the stars and planets
haze thin mist

UFO reports come in all the time. This report is from Australia:

May 17, 2002

Police see UFO

Two police officers were stunned at 5 A.M. today at Apex Park, Mildura. They both saw a silver shape in the sky and reported it immediately. "It was as if the UFO saw us. It then shot off over the river. We tried to chase it but it went in the blink of an eye," one said.

A local man reported a blue **haze** above a large water tank. A close look showed the tank had been emptied, with no sign of splashes. "UFOs seem to need water," he said. A UFO **researcher** said that UFOs are often seen over rivers and water.

UFO REPORT

On March 24, 2000, in Britain, John and Dorothy Ramsden reported a UFO that was a "lovely silver cigar shape, giving a pinkish light." For ten minutes it "hung at an angle." There were also other sightings nearby.

This photo was taken by a farmer in Peru in 1952.

Caught on camera—but what is it?

CANADA

People saw a "large craft" over mountains near Juniper, Canada, in May 2000. The UFO split into four flashing lights, like triangles. Its colors changed, flashed, and lit up the mountains. The lights joined up again before the UFO shot out of sight. Was this **ball lightning**?

MORE SIGHTINGS

UFO sightings are reported in most countries. No part of the world is free from "sky mysteries." **Surveys** show that more than half of all Americans believe UFOs have landed on Earth. Could this just be because of all the UFO movies?

Four times as many UFOs are reported in Scotland as in France and Italy. This is odd because Scotland is a smaller country. But it does have many airbases where pilots train.

About 500 UFO sightings are reported every year in Great Britain. **Researchers** say that 99 percent of all UFO reports can be explained. That leaves about five UFOs in Britain each year that are very mysterious. Maybe they are real spaceships.

UFO films have always been very popular.

buzz to fly fast and very close to something
evidence information to help prove if something is true

ENCOUNTERS OF THE FIRST KIND

Encounters of the first kind are when someone gets a close look at a UFO. Sometimes people film UFOs so they have **evidence.** Sometimes there are many witnesses, and so it seems they cannot all be lying. Can it be that all these encounters are just tricks or people's imaginations?

In 1978 a television news crew heard that a UFO had been seen in New Zealand. At midnight they filmed strange lights from their plane over the town of Kaikoura. Their **radar** screens also picked up the UFO. Suddenly, a brightly lit object flew right beside their plane. It kept pace with the plane, then zoomed ahead and disappeared.

AUSTRALIA

Chris Beacham was surfing at South Avalon Beach, near Sydney, Australia. It was an early morning in May 2000. He saw a UFO in the sky that seemed to "**buzz** three navy ships. It was silent, with a fire trail brighter than the craft itself." It remains a mystery.

Strange lights spotted over New Zealand.

radar (Radio Detection And Ranging) detecting objects through radio waves
survey investigation asking many people their views

> " The lights seemed to be in a **boomerang** shape and all white. I could not see any structure, but this thing just blocked out the sky. Its size was like a Boeing 747. "

THE HUDSON VALLEY UFO

The Hudson River Valley runs through eastern New York state. Many people saw the famous "Hudson Valley UFO" in 1982. An object seemed to hover over Yorktown, and the police switchboard became jammed with reports. It was New Year's Eve.

The first person to see lights in the sky was a retired police officer. He was in his backyard just before midnight, when he saw strange lights to the south. They were red, green, and white in a "V" shape. At first they seemed to be a jet aircraft in trouble. The lights made a faint hum and just hung in the sky.

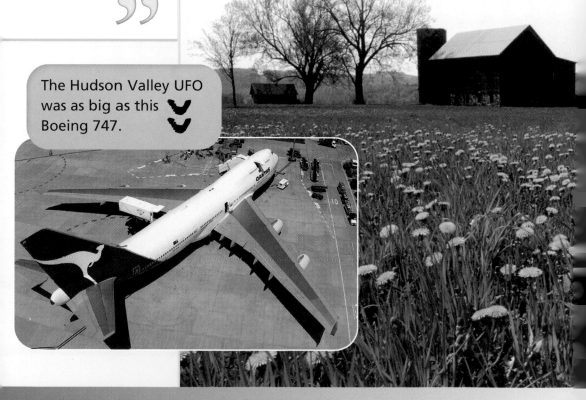

The Hudson Valley UFO was as big as this Boeing 747.

WEIRD WORDS   boomerang curved "V"-shaped, flat weapon that is thrown

UNSOLVED MYSTERY

More than 5,000 people saw the Hudson Valley UFO from 1982 to 1986. It seemed to glide over large areas, with many sightings on March 23, 1983. A guard said it was the length of three football fields. It was never seen in the day.

So what was it? Could so many people be fooled? Everyone said it looked like a huge flying machine. The only objects that move slowly and hover silently are **blimps** and hot-air balloons. But all blimp and balloon operators said that none flew at night. Maybe some **hoaxers** put lights on motorized hanggliders and flew in **formation.**

There have been many UFO sightings in the Hudson Valley.

EYEWITNESS 2

❝ The underside was dark gray with all kinds of tubes and grids. White lights were flashing with a red one in the middle. My neighbors and I stood in **awe** as it passed over without a sound. ❞

Could people really think a vehicle like this is a UFO?

formation making a shape together
hoaxers people who play tricks on others

MYSTERIES SOLVED?

UFO HUNTERS

Many groups study UFOs. They **investigate** reports from around the world. People who look at all these reports are called ufologists. They think they can soon tell if a UFO report is false, a trick, or another display from Venus.

Fog can confuse people. One woman reported seeing a glowing ball about the size of the Moon hovering over a parking lot. A UFO **investigator** checked the details and found that it really was the Moon. The woman had been fooled by fog, which made the Moon seem like a glowing object much nearer to her.

From an aircraft, a full Moon can be reflected off of oceans, lakes or wet ground. If there is a thin cloud below the aircraft, the reflection can look like a bright disk moving just under the cloud. It is as good as any special effect in a movie.

Many people have mistaken Venus for a UFO.

culprit guilty one
horizon line where the sky meets the land or sea

VENUS

Venus is the brightest planet in our night sky. Although it is over 20 million miles (32 million kilometers) away, many people report UFOs when Venus is shining. In fact, Venus is the main **culprit** in many UFO sightings.

Venus is the second planet from the Sun and is about the size of Earth. It is usually seen in the early evening near the **horizon.** Like the other planets, Venus moves slowly through the sky each month. At times it may appear to move faster and change colors. When there is fog, people are more easily confused and think Venus must be a UFO in the sky.

TRICKS OF THE LIGHT

People often report UFOs when an odd-looking cloud appears.

People also report **space junk** falling to Earth. Because it burns on reentry into the **atmosphere,** it can look like a UFO.

Flat clouds in a strange light can look just like flying saucers.

TRICK

You do not always see what you think. Is it a bird, is it a plane, or is it an alien spacecraft?

FOOLED

Some people have always liked to trick others. And some people are easily tricked. Many people want to believe in **aliens,** so they are ready to believe that fake photos are real. False pictures have been made for years.

Jokers have always made up UFO stories. Even the **CIA** has been guilty. In 1997 it admitted to telling stories about UFOs in the 1950s to cover up flight trials of top-secret spy planes that looked like giant saucers.

What is it?

For years this picture fooled some experts. It turned out to be a car's hubcap tossed up into the air.

It is easier to create fake images today with computers, but software can detect tricks quickly.

CIA United States Central Intelligence Agency

CONNED

In 1897 Alexander Hamilton came out of his house in Kansas to see a cigar-shaped UFO hovering over his farm. He said that aliens in the ship had a rope around one of his cows. This story appeared in the newspaper with statements from leading citizens telling of Hamilton's honesty. The story was believed for almost a hundred years, until an **investigator** showed it was all a **hoax.**

Hamilton was part of a jokers' club that played tricks on people. The members of the club had no idea that their lie would fool thousands of people around the world. But it did.

BEYOND ALL DOUBT

A scientist named David Simpson wanted to test UFO spotters. Would they spot a hoax? In 1970 he used a purple light to make a "close **encounter** of the first kind." UFO spotters took photos from a nearby hill and declared them "UFO beyond doubt."

Sometimes all it can take is an odd light in the sky to fool UFO spotters. ««

SR-71 BLACKBIRD

This top-secret spy plane was packed with hi-tech electronics to fool enemy radar. Its top speed was three times the speed of sound, or more than 2,200 miles (3,500 kilometers) per hour. No wonder some people panicked when it flew past.

HUMAN-MADE UFOS

When people look into the night sky and see flashing lights, they often assume there is something strange going on. But many of the moving lights up there are just planes, spacecraft, or **satellites.** A lot of UFO reports come from places with an airbase nearby. It could just be that secret aircraft being tested are mistaken for UFOs.

For years, designers have been trying to make aircraft that hover and skim through the air like Frisbees. This flat, disk shape is much better at escaping **radar** signals. Maybe some people have seen these craft being tested and thought Earth was being **invaded** by flying saucers.

The first SR-71 flew in 1966, and the U.S. Air Force still flew a few up until 1998.

Flat aircraft that take off **vertically** can look very mysterious.

remote far away from other people
satellite machine sent up to orbit Earth

AREA 51

A secret base called Area 51 is situated in the **remote** Nevada desert. Area 51 is a test site for military aircraft. In the 1950s, the U-2 spy plane was flight-tested there. A runway 6 miles (9.5 kilometers) long was used to test the F-117A Stealth Fighter. All these strange aircraft swooping through the sky sent many people running to report UFOs.

In 1986 a scientist named Robert Lazar told a television reporter that he once worked at Area 51. His job was to study a "disk-shaped flying machine." Nine such flying saucers were kept hidden at the base. Lazar believed they had not been built on Earth, but had been taken from **aliens**.

WORLD WAR II

It seems the Germans were working on disk-shaped planes in the 1940s. One called *Feuerball* could do a **vertical** take-off. Although it is unlikely these were ever used, maybe some of the flying saucers reported over the years have been human-made after all.

An early German disk-shaped plane.

vertical straight line going upward at a right angle to the ground; straight up

23

ENCOUNTERS OF THE SECOND KIND

SIGNS IN THE DESERT

Some books have been written to suggest that **aliens** visited Earth many centuries ago. They tell how spacecraft landed at special sites such as the pyramids. Maybe lines in the desert were runways for visitors from other planets.

Some people think aliens may even have built the pyramids.

A close **encounter** of the second kind is when an **alien** or UFO causes something to happen.

A REAL EFFECT

In 1957, Pedro Saucedo was driving near Levelland, Texas, when he saw a large flame ahead. His truck engine suddenly died and his lights failed. In the sky, he saw a shape like a **torpedo** about 230 feet (70 meters) long. Then it flew off at great speed. When it was gone, Pedro's lights came back on and he was able to start the engine. Fifteen other people called the police that night. They had all seen the same UFO, and their cars had all lost power. It was a real mystery.

WEIRD WORDS   crop circle large design cut into farm fields
rancher farmer who works on a cattle or sheep ranch

STRANGE EFFECTS

In 1980, a cattle **rancher** in Autstralia told how he saw a disk with a dome gliding above the ground. The UFO had orange and blue lights.

The rancher jumped on his motorcycle and sped toward the UFO. The UFO rose into the air with a sudden bang. A blast of air knocked the rancher off his motorcycle. The UFO dropped stones and plants from the sky before flying off.

A ring of black grass was left behind and 10,500 gallons (40,000 liters) had disappeared from a nearby water tank. The rancher felt sick for a week afterward. Nobody could explain what happened in this close encounter of the second kind.

SIGNS IN THE CORN

Could strange patterns left in fields be the work of UFOs? Some people say **crop circles** are flattened by the weight of a flying saucer landing in a field. Other shapes may be the marks left by a UFO's jet engines.

Are all crop circles human-made?

RENDLESHAM FOREST, SUFFOLK

The forest is on the east coast of Britain. U.S. airbases have been in this area since World War II. It is a good position for keeping watch across the North Sea to Russia. Whatever happened there, it remains a place of secrets.

WOODBRIDGE AIRBASE, ENGLAND

On a December night in 1980, two U.S. Air Force officers were guarding Woodbridge airbase in Rendlesham Forest. They suddenly saw a light moving above the trees. It looked like a plane was in trouble. The guards called the control tower. They were told that there were no **radar** signals and no aircraft were flying. More guards arrived and they found a glowing object in a forest clearing. The object stood on three legs, was silver, and had a red light on top. As the guards went nearer, the object began to glide away. Nearby farm animals went into a panic. The guards were shocked, too. What was it?

DEPARTMENT OF THE AIR FORCE
HEADQUARTERS DIST COMBAT SUPPORT GROUP (USAFE)

The next day there were three deep, round marks in the ground. The marks were **radioactive.** More lights came over the area the next night. Many people saw objects moving in the sky. I witnessed them, too.

Charles Halt Lt Col. USAF

Charles Halt Lt Col. USAF
Deputy Base Commander

This is an extract from the official report. **‹‹**

radioactive giving off radiation (electromagnetic energy waves)

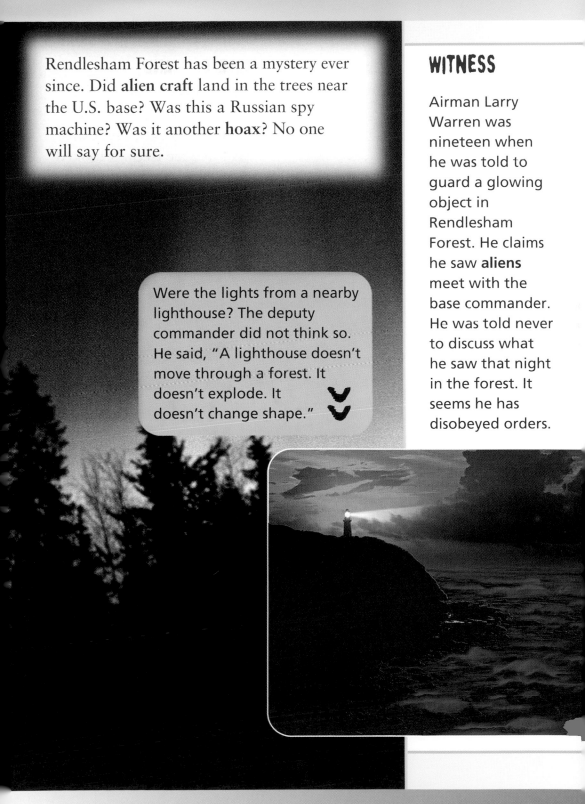

Rendlesham Forest has been a mystery ever since. Did **alien craft** land in the trees near the U.S. base? Was this a Russian spy machine? Was it another **hoax**? No one will say for sure.

Airman Larry Warren was nineteen when he was told to guard a glowing object in Rendlesham Forest. He claims he saw **aliens** meet with the base commander. He was told never to discuss what he saw that night in the forest. It seems he has disobeyed orders.

Were the lights from a nearby lighthouse? The deputy commander did not think so. He said, "A lighthouse doesn't move through a forest. It doesn't explode. It doesn't change shape."

RADAR

Radar picks up radio waves to give pilots information. It was first developed in the 1930s. Now it can tell the size of an object, its speed, and its distance. Air traffic control uses radar to track planes. **NASA** uses radar to track **satellites, space junk,** and UFOs.

ENCOUNTERS IN THE SKY

This message came to a pilot from Iran's military control center in Teheran: "Bright lights in the sky. **Investigate.**" He took off in a Phantom fighter jet at 1:20 A.M. on September 19, 1976:

> **Pilot report**
> I saw a glow in the sky miles ahead. As I got close, I saw an object zoom away. Just as my radar showed something big, systems on my **instrument panel** lost power. I turned back to base in a panic and the electricity returned. What a relief!

So what was in the sky over Iran that night? A freak effect of the weather? Spies testing secret aircraft? **Aliens**? Will we ever know?

Radar should pick up everything in the sky.

instrument panel dials and gauges a pilot uses to fly an aircraft

A SCARY ENCOUNTER

The Nullarbor Plain stretches for hundreds of miles across Australia. The Knowles family was driving across this desert one night in 1988. This is their story:

In the middle of nowhere, a glowing light came down over our car. A loud noise above us shook us all over the road. Black dust gushed into the car window and a foul smell made us sick.

Suddenly the car left the ground. We rose into the air before falling with a crash that burst a tire. The exhaust cracked on the road. We swerved to a halt, ran out, and hid in bushes until the object flew away. We were terrified. No one believed us.

VISIBLE EFFECTS

Tests on the Knowles' car showed:

- Marks on the roof as if the car had been lifted.
- The speedometer was jammed at 125 miles (200 kilometers) per hour.
- A fine, gray, unknown powder was all over the car.

Mrs. Knowles had a rash where the dust had touched her.

NEXT 96 km

Kangaroos may roam the huge Nullarbor Plain, but what about aliens?

NASA National Aeronautics and Space Administration
(The U.S. space program and organization)

OTHER ENCOUNTERS

CLOSE ENCOUNTERS OF THE THIRD KIND

This famous movie from 1977 was director Steven Spielberg's first movie after *Jaws.* It was originally going to be called *Watch the Skies.* It was the first of many impressive Spielberg UFO **science fiction** movies. Its message was "We are not alone."

Encounters of the third kind involve people seeing or meeting **aliens.** Encounters of the fourth kind involve people being taken by aliens.

ALIENS
Today, books and movies are full of alien stories. Just over 50 years ago, hardly anyone thought about aliens. Now they have become a huge business. Some people believe aliens often make contact and kidnap humans. Many believe that **governments** try to keep information about aliens hidden to prevent mass panic.

EARLY ENCOUNTER 1
One of the first reports of a meeting with an alien came in 1952. George Adamski told of his close encounter of the third kind. He met a UFO pilot in the desert. Or so he said. The world was hooked.

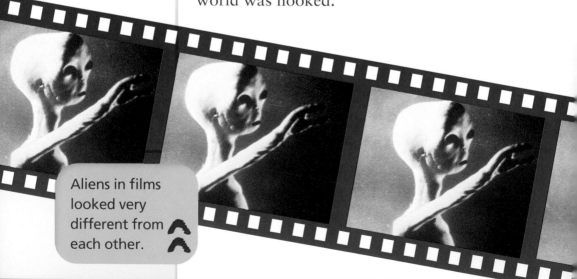

Aliens in films looked very different from each other.

extraterrestrial beyond Earth, or a being from outer space (in science fiction)

WHAT DO ALIENS LOOK LIKE?

People who claim to have had encounters of the third kind often describe aliens as being "like humans." They say aliens have large heads, big eyes, and slit mouths. Their skin is said to be silver or gray. But is this just because that is how aliens often appear in movies?

EARLY ENCOUNTER 2

In 1954, Jennie Roetenberg said she and her children saw a silver saucer hovering above their house in Britain:

> "There were two 'men' looking out through windows in the side of the ship. They had high foreheads and wore blue outfits with clear helmets. They seemed to be watching me almost sadly."

E.T.

This 1982 movie about an **extraterrestrial** shows the friendly side of aliens. A ten-year-old boy named Eliot makes friends with a visitor from outer space. He helps the alien to return home. Steven Spielberg also directed this popular Disney movie. It made over $750 million.

One of the most famous movie aliens is Yoda from *Star Wars.*

TAKEN

Most victims report:

- a bright light;
- being confused;
- waking in a strange room;
- being **examined**;
- getting a warning or information from aliens;
- waking up "back in the real world";
- losing their memory for a few days.

Steven Michalek was ill for many days, but doctors could not explain it. >>

FRIENDS OR FOES?

Hundreds of people each year say they meet friendly "**extraterrestrials**." Other people describe being taken into a spacecraft against their will. This is called an **encounter** of the fourth kind. Some people are never seen again.

The United States, Canada, Australia, and Britain have filed many reports of **alien** encounters. India and China have very few. But can these reports really be true? Do aliens really visit some parts of the world more than others?

Steven Michalek told of an encounter of the third kind when he saw a UFO at Falcon Lake in Canada in 1967. He looked inside and came away with strange burns on his body.

abduction kidnapping
examine to inspect and look very closely

The following report of an **abduction** is more recent. Nothing is said about how the man got away, so it does not seem **reliable**:

ALIEN ABDUCTION FILE

Place: Taralgon, Victoria, Australia
Year: 2002

Name: Martin Taylor

Age: 43

Statement:

"I was out walking when a blue light blinded me and I fell down dizzy. I woke up on a large metal table in a round room. I was strapped down and there were wires attached to my arms, neck, and head. A figure with very large almond-shaped eyes and almost see-through skin stood over me. It spoke in a strange language."

Many people claiming to have been abducted by aliens report strange, glowing lights. >>

Twenty-five-year-old Bob Simon was asleep when he was suddenly pulled toward his bedroom window. He awoke to see a gray alien with red eyes and huge hands. Simon grabbed a small knife and the alien let go of him. A real encounter, or just a bad dream?

BETTY AND BARNEY HILL

Does their story stand up?

- An airbase did track an unknown object at that time and place.
- Under **hypnosis,** they both told stories with identical details.
- Betty could draw a map of the stars to show where the aliens lived.

Betty and Barney Hill explain a picture they drew of the craft that followed them. **>>**

WHEN TIME STANDS STILL

People who say they have met **aliens** often tell how they lost all sense of time. Perhaps they were in a **trance.**

Betty and Barney Hill were among the first to speak about meeting aliens. They were driving in the White Mountains near the U.S./Canadian border in 1961. A bright light followed them. They stopped the car and Barney said he saw "a craft." He saw aliens' heads through the window. He drove away, but realized they had lost an hour. Where had the time gone? In her sleep, Betty dreamed of being taken onto the craft for tests. Her story hit the news. It was later made into a television movie called *The UFO Incident.*

Police Report: 1973
Pascagoula, Mississippi

Calvin Parker (19) and
Charles Hickson (42) arrived
at the police station in a
state of shock. Both men
told me they had just
escaped from an alien
spacecraft. They had not been drinking.

Does Hickson and Parker's story stand up? **‹‹**

The men said that while they were fishing in
the river, a UFO landed and three aliens came
out. Parker described them as having bullet-shaped
heads, no necks, and no eyes. Hickson said they
had slits for mouths, gray skin, round feet, and
clawlike hands.

The two men were taken against their will to the
UFO for medical tests. Half an hour later, the men
were released.
Could be a **hoax**. Will need to **investigate** further.

- The police put the two men in a **bugged** room. Instead of talking about a hoax, one of them prayed.
- Experts looked at the site and tested the two men. They said they believed them.

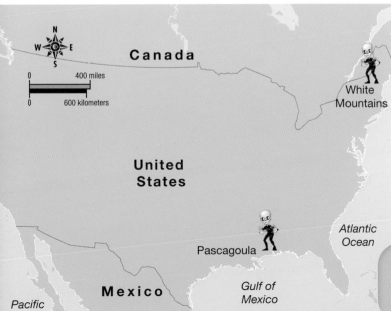

Where the Hills and Hickson and Parker saw aliens. **‹‹**

hypnosis controlling the mind through a trance or deep sleep
trance in a sleeplike state

AMAZING STORY

Travis Walton wrote a book about his close **encounter**. It was called *Fire in the Sky*. A movie was made in 1993. Since the movie, Travis has passed two more lie-detector tests. He has not had **hypnosis,** since he is afraid of the memories it might bring back.

FIRE IN THE SKY

This encounter happened in Sitgreaves National Forest, Arizona, on November 6, 1975:

Last night at 6.00P.M. we were driving through the forest. There were seven of us in the truck and we had just finished work. Suddenly we all saw a huge disk hovering over the trees. Mike stopped the truck and for some reason Travis got out to get a closer look.

The disk had a yellow glow, and as Travis got near, a flash of blue light knocked him flat. Mike put his foot down and we got the heck out of there. I said,"Hey, shouldn't we get Travis?", but Mike kept driving. We went straight to the police.

A scene from the film *Fire in the Sky.*

THE INCREDIBLE ACCOUNT OF ONE MAN'S ABDUCTION BY A UFO
THE WALTON EXPERIENCE

0-425-03675-8 • $1.95 • A BERKLEY BOOK

By Travis Walton
With full details on the Medical, Legal and Psychological Investigations of the Arizona Incident.

lie detector machine that records a person's reactions during questioning to see if he or she is lying

MYSTERIOUS ENCOUNTER

The police searched the forest, but there was no sign of Travis. Maybe the other men had murdered Travis and used the UFO as a cover story. But a **lie detector** showed they were all telling the truth. So where was Travis?

Five days later, Travis called his sister. He was a few miles away, naked and confused. He told a story of **aliens** who had kidnapped him. They were nearly his height with hairless heads. Each one had large eyes, tiny ears, and a slit for a mouth. They had done many tests on him. He also said he was shown a control room, where he could look out at the stars.

Travis Walton said aliens had done tests on him.

ray narrow beam of light

THE BEAM OF LIGHT

In 1993 Kelly Cahill and her family were driving in Australia. It was late at night. Suddenly a bright light shone down on them. Kelly was scared. The next thing she knew, she was waking up in a **daze**. Her husband and children did not know what had happened, either.

BEINGS FROM THE SKY

Later at home, Kelly saw strange marks on her body. She felt ill with stomach pains for two weeks. In a few days she began to remember. She saw the events of that night like a movie. It started as their car stopped. She and her husband got out. They walked past another parked car, toward the UFO.

IS IT LIKELY?

If there are such things as aliens:
- Would they just pop out from UFOs every so often in **remote** areas?
- Would they really grab a few humans to **examine** and then let them go again?
- Would they come all that way from outer space just for a brief **encounter**?

This painting was based on Kelly's description of her encounter.

daze state of sleepy confusion
hallucinate see things that are not really there

MEMORY

Kelly told her story and experts did tests. None of them could explain what she said. Was it all a dream?

> "I came to a group of **aliens.** They were taller than me, with large, red eyes. One flew over to me and I screamed and passed out. The next thing I knew, I was waking up in the car an hour later.
> "In my dreams, I remembered one of the aliens stooping over me. It kissed me—where I later found the marks on my body."

Then witnesses came forward. People in the car parked nearby said they had seen what happened and it was just as Kelly had described.

MEETINGS

Stories about meeting aliens may not always be as they seem:

- There may be other reasons for such stories.
- There may be missing details that have not been told.

People can sometimes **hallucinate,** especially if they have a fever. They may "see" things that are not really there. ◀◀

ENCOUNTERS WITH THE MEN IN BLACK

Victims often report:

- being alone when they visit;
- that the men's black clothes always look new;
- strange smells after the visit;
- feeling ill afterward.

They often arrive in an old, yet gleaming black car.

VISITORS

Aliens are said to come in all shapes and sizes. Sometimes they are silver or gray. Sometimes they are tall with big heads. Sometimes they are "little green men." We all have our own idea of what aliens look like. But what about "men in black"? Some people say they must be aliens as well.

MIB

It all started in the 1960s. An American UFO expert said strange men in dark suits came to threaten him. They did not like him studying aliens and UFOs. Other people tell of **officials** who warned them to keep quiet about UFO **encounters.** They think these men in black are from a secret **government** department.

officials people with authority, having special duties

THE MYSTERY CALL

In 1976 Dr. Hopkins was alone at home in Maine. He had been investigating UFOs. He told how a stranger visited and asked to come in. The man was dressed in black, and when he took off his hat, he was totally hairless. His face was very pale except for lipstick around his mouth. He smeared his mouth by mistake and there were no lips underneath.

The man in black asked Dr. Hopkins questions about UFOs, but he already knew the answers. Then his voice slowed down and he said, "My energy is running low. Must go now. Goodbye." He left the house, turned a corner, and vanished in a flash of light.

MEN IN BLACK – THE MOVIES

Stories about aliens that want to destroy us can be scary or funny. In the *Men in Black* movies the MIB are humans who rid Earth of alien threats. They work for a secret government department that tracks down friendly and not-so-friendly aliens.

CRASHING TO EARTH

DR. HYNEK

One of the experts called in to **examine** Mantell's crashed plane was Dr. Hynek. At first, he did not believe in UFOs. But he has since become a believer and leading UFO expert.

Hynek was an adviser for the movie *Close Encounters of the Third Kind.*

There are still big questions about UFOs and **aliens**:

- Why has an alien spacecraft never been shot down?
- How is it that UFOs have never broken down, left bits behind, or crashed?
- Has anyone been killed by aliens?

But maybe all of these things have actually happened. The next few pages look at the **evidence** for and against UFO crash reports.

CLOSE ENCOUNTER
OF THE FIRST KIND
Sighting of a UFO

CLOSE ENCOUNTER
OF THE SECOND KIND
Physical Evidence

CLOSE ENCOUNTER
OF THE THIRD KIND
Contact

WE ARE NOT ALONE

CLOSE ENCOUNTERS
OF THE THIRD KIND

MYSTERY CRASHES

In 1948 a UFO was said to have caused a death. Thomas Mantell was an expert pilot who took off to **investigate** a UFO report. His last radio message said he was taking a closer look at the object in the sky ahead of him. Then, for some reason, his plane fell from the sky. The crash remained a real mystery.

WEIRD WORDS   gorge narrow, rocky valley or ravine
leak release secret information on purpose

RUSSIAN MYSTERY

In 1991 **rumors** came from Russia of a huge UFO. Fighter jets chased a large object in the sky, but it got away. People in the Tien Shan Mountains said a large object had fallen into a deep, **remote gorge**. A search party set off to see if the story was true.

> **Tien Shan Mountains Search party report:**
> At last we're near the crash site. We can see a wreck, but there's no way we can get near. Electrical energy is buzzing all around. All our watches have just stopped. This place is **radioactive**.

The party had to give up, but they returned to the site the next year. By then the crashed UFO had disappeared.

This information was reported to have been **leaked** from a secret army security source:

> **TOP SECRET**
> Four officers see strange object crash in Mexico—38 miles (61 kilometers) south of Laredo, Texas. Bodies recovered from scene.

THOMAS MANTELL FLE

Roswell Army Airbase now has the disk reported by a local **rancher**. The flying object landed on a ranch near Roswell last week. The disk was picked up at the ranch. It was inspected at the Roswell Army Airbase.

THE ROSWELL MYSTERY

The name of the Roswell Airbase in New Mexico has become world famous. It is known for a strange event in 1947. But it has been full of mystery ever since. How much of the story is pure fiction? How much is still secret? Roswell is said by some people to be part of the biggest cover-up of all time.

RUMORS

The U.S. Army agreed that a flying object had been "picked up." But local people spoke of a crash. Some had seen a glowing object fall from the sky and crash in a field. The real mystery had only just begun.

The crash made the front page of newspapers. ❯❯

The crash site was tested for **radioactive** debris. ❯❯

ll Daily Record

Business Office 2288
News Department 2287

ROSWELL, NEW MEXICO, TUESDAY, JULY 8, 1947

5c PER COPY.

RAAF Captures Flying Saucer On Ranch in Roswell Region

House Passes Tax Slash by Large Margin

Defeat Amendment By Demos to Remove Many from Rolls

Security Council Paves Way to Talks On Arms Reductions

No Details of Flying Disk Are Revealed

Roswell Hardware Man and Wife Report Disk Seen

Ex-King Carol Weds Mme. Lupescu

Former King Carol of Romania and Mme. Elena Lupescu in May, 1941. A member of Carol's household in Rio de Janeiro said the ex king and his companion for 23 years in reign and exile were recently married at their hotel Copacabana Palace suite. (AP Wirephoto)

Miners and Operators Sign Highest Wage Pact in History

debris scattered fragments after a crash

TRYING TO FIND THE TRUTH

Rumors spread about the army hiding a crashed flying saucer in a secret **hangar.** Then there were reports about **debris** from the crash. A witness said it was made from "nothing on this Earth and covered with weird writing."

Locals said they watched in horror as bodies of many **aliens** were found in the wreck. The army denied all the stories. The UFO was said to be no more than a weather balloon. But over 50 years later, many people still believe that the Roswell crash proved aliens really exist and that **governments** try to keep the proof hidden. Then again, it could all have been a great **hoax.**

THE PLOT THICKENS

In 1995 some film turned up. It was meant to show the dead aliens for all to see. But were they really aliens? Maybe the film was made to keep the world from finding out the truth. It was probably just another hoax.

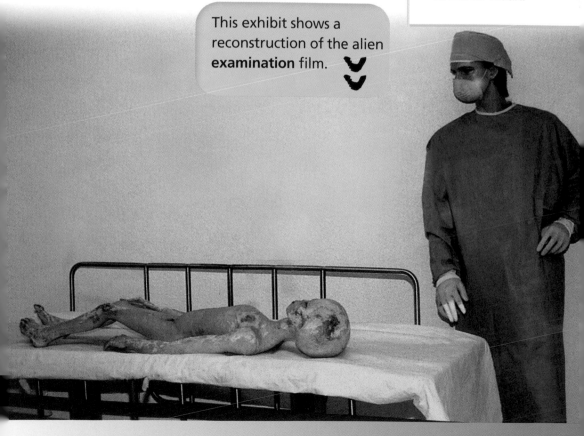

This exhibit shows a reconstruction of the alien **examination** film. ❱❱

hangar large shed for housing aircraft

BIG BANG MYSTERY

It was the biggest crash of the 20th century.
Something huge fell from the sky on June 30,
1908. The heat and shock waves were felt
hundreds of miles away. The explosion was
massive. It was like a **nuclear** bomb. Or was
it a nuclear-powered spaceship that crashed?

SIBERIA

The **impact** was in a forest in Siberia. The area
was called Tunguska. In the town of Vanavara,
40 miles (64 kilometers) from the blast, people
were knocked over. Windows smashed, and the
bang was heard 500 miles (800 kilometers) away.
A train 375 miles (600 kilometers) from the blast
was nearly shaken off the track. Luckily, no one
was killed.

asteroid rock that orbits the Sun—like a small planet;
up to 600 miles (965 kilometers) across

FLATTENED FOREST

It took years for scientists to find the **remote** crash site. They were shocked. They expected to find **debris.** They thought there would be a huge **crater.** What they found were trees thrown down like matchsticks. In the center, trees with no bark or branches were still standing. Locals had seen an oval shape moving across the sky just before the impact. So what was it?

Most scientists thought it was a **meteorite** or a **comet.** Perhaps it exploded before it hit the ground, so there was no crater. Others spoke of **asteroids.** But some whispered about **alien craft.** They still do.

Trees at the crash site were flattened. >>

If a large meteorite had hit the ground, it would have left a huge crater. But there was nothing.

> 66
> I felt a great heat, as if my shirt had caught fire. There was a bang in the sky and a mighty crash. I was thrown from the porch and I blacked out. The sky opened and a hot wind blew, as if from a cannon.
> 99
>
> A witness at Kirensk, 1908.

impact one thing coming into contact with another with force
nuclear having to do with atomic reactions

SCANNING THE SKIES

THE WAR OF THE WORLDS

The writer H.G. Wells wrote a science-fiction book in 1898 about aliens from Mars **invading** Earth. The actor Orson Welles broadcast a radio play of *The War of the Worlds* in the United States in 1938. There was mass panic. People listening thought aliens really had landed in New Jersey.

Space and its mysteries will always amaze us. The world above our heads will always get our imaginations going. We have always wanted to know about life on other planets. The mysteries out there will keep **science fiction** going for years to come.

SCIENCE FICTION TO SCIENCE FACT

This book is full of people's mysterious stories. Some are hard to believe, but people have still told them. We can only wonder if they were telling lies, or if they were mistaken in some way. Then again, maybe they were telling the truth!

Maybe science can help us find out what is out there.

pulsar star that gives off radio pulses as it spins

SETI

In 1960 scientists began searching with the SETI (Search for **Extraterrestrial** Intelligence) program. SETI now scans millions of radio waves every second. Computers sort natural signals from those that might be from **aliens.** At one time the radio pulses from **pulsars** were thought to be signals from aliens.

We now have radio telescopes to scan the skies in extraterrestrial research. The new Allen Telescope in California will be used only for SETI research. Other scientists plan to send signals for aliens to pick up. A few think that is a bad idea because we might attract unwanted attention. It might start the events shown in *The War of the Worlds* or *Independence Day*.

INDEPENDENCE DAY

In this movie, aliens hover in their massive spacecraft over major cities and finally attack Earth. Almost everything is destroyed. The few human survivors have to fight back.

Independence Day earned more money than any other movie in 1996.

THE SKY'S THE LIMIT

If **aliens** visit Earth, it is unlikely they will be from our **solar system.** We must look at other stars in our **galaxy.** There are 100 galaxies within 21 light years of Earth. A light year is how far light can travel in one year. That is almost 6 million million miles (10 million million kilometers). Some of these galaxies could be the home of a visiting UFO. The possibilities seem to be endless.

We used to think aliens came from Mars, as in *The War of the Worlds.* **NASA** thinks there may well be life there. But they say, "We're not talking about 'little green men.' These are small single-cells. There's no **evidence** that any **higher life form** ever existed on Mars."

bacteria tiny living things made up of single cells
fossil ancient remains of life found in soil and rock

THE FUTURE

Mars will be the focus of much research in the 21st century. Mars is the planet in our solar system that is most similar to Earth. In 1996 NASA scientists thought they had proof of **fossils** on Mars. They may be the remains of **bacteria.** Not everyone is sure, but missions to Mars should soon find out. Both the United States and Britain sent robots to Mars in 2003. There may even be astronauts sent one day. Who knows what mysterious **encounters** there will be? Perhaps, as we travel in space, humans will one day be the aliens!

THE TRUTH, AS THEY SAY, IS OUT THERE....

WOULD YOU BELIEVE IT?

- According to a **survey** by a UFO website, 21 percent of humans say they have been taken into a UFO.
- Over 50 percent of people who answered the survey said they had seen a UFO.

This might tell us more about people who read UFO websites than it does about UFOs!

We have barely started to explore our own galaxy. Who knows what is out there? **《**

galaxy star system in space
solar system group of planets that orbit the Sun

51

FIND OUT MORE

ALIEN WEBSITES

LIFE ON MARS
Infomation about the SETI project and photos of the mysterious faces and signs on Mars.
activemind.com/Mysterious

NASA
The latest news on alien-hunting technology and human-made UFOs.
nasa.gov/

BBC SCIENCE
Includes information on the hunt for life on Mars and plans for future space exploration.
bbc.co.uk/science

BOOKS

Campbell, Peter A. *Alien Encounters*. Brookfield, Conn.: Millbrook Press, 2000.

Elfman, Eric *et al. Almanac of Alien Encounters*. New York: Random House, 2001.

Oxlade, Chris. *Can Science Solve? The Mystery of Life on Other Planets*. City: Heinemann Library, 2002.

Oxlade, Chris, and Ganeri, Anita. *Can Science Solve? The Mystery of UFOs*. City: Heinemann Library, 1999.

WORLD WIDE WEB

If you want to find out more about mysterious encounters, you can search the Internet using keywords such as these:

- Roswell mystery
- Tunguska explosion
- life + Mars
- Area 51
- UFO + [name of your state]

You can also find your own keywords by using headings or words from this book. Use the search tips below to help you find the most useful websites.

SEARCH TIPS

There are billions of pages on the Internet, so it can be difficult to find exactly what you are looking for. If you just type in "alien" on a search engine such as Google, you'll get a list of over eight million web pages. These search skills will help you find useful websites more quickly:

- Know exactly what you want to find out.
- Use simple keywords instead of whole sentences.
- Use two to six keywords in a search.
- Be precise—only use names of people, places, or things.
- If you want to find words that go together, put quote marks around them.
- Use the "+" sign to add certain words.

WHERE TO LOOK

SEARCH ENGINE

A search engine looks through the entire web and lists all the sites that match your keywords. It can give thousands of links, but the best matches are at the top of the list. Try **google.com**.

SEARCH DIRECTORY

This is more like a library of websites that have been sorted by a person instead of a computer. You can search by keyword or subject. A good example is **yahooligans.com**.

GLOSSARY

abduction kidnapping

alien creature from a faraway place or another planet

alien craft spaceships flown by creatures from another planet

asteroid rock that orbits the Sun like a small planet; up to 600 miles (965 kilometers) across

astronomer someone who studies the stars and planets

atmosphere gases surrounding a planet

awe shock, amazement, and wonder

bacteria very tiny living things made up of single cells

being living creature

blimp large, gas-filled airship

boomerang curved "V"-shaped flat weapon that is thrown

bug hidden microphone

buzz to fly fast and very close to something

CIA United States Central Intelligence Agency

comet moving body in space with a bright head and long tail

cover-up effort to keep something from being made public

crater hole in the ground made by the impact of a meteorite

crop circle large design cut into a farm field

culprit guilty one

daze state of sleepy confusion

debris scattered fragments after a crash

encounter meeting, especially an unexpected one

evidence information to help prove if something is true

examine to inspect and look very closely

extraterrestrial beyond Earth, or a being from outer space (in science fiction)

formation making a shape together

fossil ancient remains of life found in soil and rock

galaxy star system in space

gorge narrow, rocky valley

government group of leaders in charge of running a country

hallucinate to see things that are not really there

hangar large shed for housing aircraft

haze thin mist

higher life form any creature that moves and feeds

hoax joke, trick, or something that is not real

hoaxer person who play tricks on others

horizon line where the sky meets the land or water

hypnosis   controlling the mind through a trance or deep sleep

impact   one thing coming into contact with another with force

instrument panel   dials and gauges a pilot uses to fly an aircraft

invade   to enter somewhere and take over

investigate   study carefully in great detail

investigator   someone who checks out the details to get to the truth

leak   release secret information on purpose

lie detector   machine that records a person's reactions during questioning to see if he or she is lying

meteorite   lump of rock, metal, or matter from outer space

NASA   National Aeronautics and Space Administration (U.S. space organization)

nuclear   having to do with atomic reactions

officials   people with authority, having special duties

prehistoric   thousands of years ago, before all written records

pulsar   star that gives off radio pulses as it spins

radar   method of detecting objects through radio waves (Radio Detection And Ranging)

radioactive   giving off radiation (electromagnetic energy waves)

rancher   farmer who works on a cattle or sheep ranch

reliable   can be trusted

remote   far away from other people

researcher   someone who finds out information about a subject

rumor   information from gossip that may not be true

satellite   machine sent up to orbit Earth and send back information

science fiction   made-up stories that may twist the facts of science

solar system   group of stars and planets that orbit the Sun

space junk   bits of old satellites and spacecraft left to float in space

survey   investigation asking many people their views

torpedo   cigar-shaped underwater missile

trance   in a sleeplike state

unidentified   something that cannot be named or explained

vast   huge; enormously big

vertical   straight line going upward at a right angle to the ground; straight up

waterspout   twisting column of water that acts like a tornado over a sea, ocean, or lake

INDEX